Disney
Winnie the Pooh
STORYBOOK COLLECTION

Disney PRESS

New York

Table of Contents

by
Piglet

Winnie the Pooh is based on the "Winnie the Pooh" works by A.A. Milne and E.H. Shepard.
Stories written by Thea Feldman and Catherine Hapka. Illustrated by the Disney Storybook Artists.

Copyright © 2012 Disney Enterprises, Inc. All rights reserved.
Printed in the United States of America

First Edition

10 9 8 7 6 5 4 3 2 1

FAC-038091-15251

This book is set in 18-point Goudy Infant.

ISBN 978-1-4231-6540-8

For more Disney Press fun, visit www.disneybooks.com

Disney
Winnie the Pooh
A Portrait of
Friendship

by
Piglet

iglet painted pictures of everything in the Hundred-Acre Wood. He painted the tall, leafy trees. And the bright, yellow sun. And flowers of every size and color.

One day Piglet decided he wanted to paint what he loved best of all in the Wood: his friends!

Piglet asked Pooh, Rabbit, Kanga, Roo, and the rest of his friends if they would each sit for a portrait.

"I'd be honored!" said Pooh. Everyone else felt the same way.

The next day, Piglet set up his studio outside in the sunshine. He was ready to begin with Pooh.

Piglet soon saw Pooh heading his way, but he walked right by.

"Pooh, wait!" cried Piglet. "It's time to sit for your portrait."

"Oh, is that now?" Pooh asked. "I thought it was time to fill up my honeypot—and my tummy."

Pooh didn't want to let down his friend. "All right, Piglet," he said. "You can paint my picture now.

"I'm sure my tummy can wait," he added, though he was not at all certain.

"Now try to sit still, Pooh," Piglet said.

Pooh did. But his tummy did not. It **rumbled** to the left and it **rumbled** to the right.

Finally, Pooh's tummy **rumbled** him up onto his feet.

"Sorry, Piglet, but perhaps now is not a good time to sit still after all," said Pooh as he picked up his honeypot and followed his tummy.

Piglet tried painting Rabbit next. He worked for a few
minutes, then gave Rabbit a bunch of carrots to hold.

"These remind me of my garden," said Rabbit, jumping
up. "And my garden reminds me that I have work to do. I'm sorry,
Piglet, but we'll have to finish another time." Rabbit hurried off.

Tigger had no trouble with Piglet painting his picture. The trouble was all Piglet's, since Tigger couldn't stop bouncing with excitement. "Sorry, Pigalet, but bouncing is what tiggers do best!" Tigger cried.

While Piglet waited for Tigger to stop bouncing, Kanga and Roo arrived. They were excited to have their family portrait painted.

But Tigger was so excited to see Roo,
he snatched up his little buddy and the
two **bounced** off into the Wood.

Piglet had much better luck with Eeyore, who sat as still and as gray as a rock.

"Eeyore, yours is the only portrait I've been able to finish," said Piglet.

"That's too bad," said Eeyore.

"Everyone else had too much to do," said Piglet.

"I'm just doing what I always do, too. Not much," said Eeyore.

Then he lumbered off to do not much somewhere else.

13

Piglet thought for a moment. "That's it!" he cried. "I need to paint my friends doing what they *always* do!"

Piglet packed up his art supplies and went to find Pooh. He painted Pooh following a bee.

Buzz

Then he painted several
bees following Pooh.

Buzzzzzzzzzzz

Piglet especially liked the painting he did of Pooh finally
getting a smackerel of honey.

Piglet went to Rabbit's garden next. Instead of asking Rabbit to stay still, he stood and painted while his subject moved about in his garden.

He painted several wonderful scenes of Rabbit at work.

As for Tigger, it gave Piglet a bit of a headache to follow his **bouncing** with his eyes. But he finally managed to paint Tigger's portrait.

Thump!

Piglet couldn't wait to show everyone his portraits. He invited his friends to view them.

Pooh and the others walked around and looked at one painting after another. They were very silent, which was unusual. Piglet began to worry.

Did his friends not like his artwork?

Finally, Pooh cleared his throat. "I'd like to say how wonderful your paintings are, Piglet." Then he looked thoughtful. "I'd also like to apologize."

"Whatever for, Pooh?" asked Piglet.
"For saying I'd sit still for you and
then, well, not sitting still," said Pooh.
Everyone else agreed with Pooh.
Everyone except Eeyore.

"Thank you," Piglet said, "but sitting still isn't what *anybody* does best." He looked at Eeyore. "Except Eeyore, that is."

Piglet continued, "Everyone is good at something different. My paintings show you all doing the something you love best.

"And they will always remind me," he added, "of how lucky I am to have so many unique and wonderful friends!"

![Disney Winnie the Pooh]

Hide and Pooh Seek

Ii was a lovely spring day in the Hundred-Acre Wood. "A nice day like this calls for a game," Christopher Robin declared.

"A game? What sort of game?" asked Winnie the Pooh.

Christopher Robin smiled. "Let's play hide-and-go-seek!"

"Hide and go what now?" Rabbit asked.

"One of us closes his eyes and counts to one hundred," Christopher Robin explained. "Meanwhile, the rest of us hide."

Christopher Robin tugged gently on Pooh's ear.

"Tag—you're It, Pooh Bear!"

Pooh rubbed his ear. "What is it that I am, exactly?"

Now, Pooh was a bear of very little brain. But he soon figured out what was happening. He was supposed to cover his eyes, count to one hundred, and then find his friends.

"I know the perfect hiding place," he said, licking his lips hungrily. "The honey tree!" He rushed to the honey tree.

"Aha! Found you!" he cried.

Pooh looked around in surprise. The bees were there.
The honey was there. But his friends were not!

Pooh thought about helping himself to some honey.
But then he had another thought.

"They must be hiding in Rabbit's garden!"
Pooh said.

But Pooh's friends weren't hiding
in Rabbit's garden.

They also weren't in Pooh's favorite
spot in the meadow, where he liked to
lie and watch the clouds.

Or in his comfy bed.

Or even at his Thoughtful
Spot. "Oh, bother!" Pooh said.

Just then Kanga came by. "Do you know where Roo is,
Pooh?" she asked.

"Well, I know where he's not," Pooh said. "He's not in
any of my favorite spots."

Kanga chuckled. "That's no surprise," she said kindly.
"Roo has lots of his own favorite spots."

Pooh realized Kanga was right. He'd searched his favorite places. But if he wanted to find his friends, he had to check *their* favorite places!

Pooh went straight to the hollow log near Piglet's house. He peered inside—and there was Piglet!

"I'm glad you found me, Pooh," Piglet admitted. "It's awfully dark in here."

"Will you help me find the others?" Pooh asked. "Let's figure out where Roo might like to hide."

Together, Pooh and Piglet found Roo hiding—and playing—in the sandy pit.

They all figured out that Tigger might be hiding in his favorite bouncing spot.

Then they found
Rabbit in his cornfield,
picking corn while
he hid there.

Eeyore was in his favorite thistle patch. Owl was there, too.

"I must finish my story later," Owl told Eeyore
as they joined the others.

"Yes, I suppose you must," Eeyore said
with a sigh.

Finally, only Christopher Robin was missing.

"Oh, dear," Piglet said. "What if we never find him?"

"We probably won't," Eeyore said, sounding gloomy.

Then Pooh remembered something.
"Christopher Robin likes to climb trees,"
he said. "Let's look . . . up!"

They all looked up. "There he is!"
Roo cried. "You were right, Pooh!"

Christopher Robin climbed down from his hiding spot. "Well done, Pooh Bear," he said.

"Let's play again!" Tigger cried. "This time, Piglet's It!"

As Piglet began counting, the others all hurried off to find hiding spots.

"Where will you hide, Pooh?" Christopher Robin asked.

"The honey tree, of course," Pooh said. "Piglet will know exactly how to find me there."

Christopher Robin laughed. "Silly old bear!"

Disney
Winnie the Pooh

The Sweetest of Friends

"Good morning, Piglet."

"Good morning, Pooh."

It was another day in the Hundred-Acre Wood.
That meant it was another day for best friends Pooh
and Piglet to be together.

"Pooh, I made some haycorn pie," said Piglet.

"Mmmm," said Pooh. "That will go lovely with some honey on top."

The two friends sat down and had a bite to eat.

When the last drop of sweet, sticky honey had disappeared inside Pooh's tummy, he stood up.

"It feels like nap time," he said, as he usually did after having a sizable smackerel of honey.

Piglet answered, "I think a nap is a splendid idea, Pooh—
but perhaps you could be persuaded to take a walk first?"

Pooh stretched and yawned. "Lead the way, Piglet,"
said Pooh.

This morning was not unlike any other. Each day was a different adventure.

In the fall, Pooh and Piglet played in piles of leaves.

In the winter, they made snow angels.

In the spring, they watched as the Hundred-Acre Wood became green again.

In the summer, they picked fragrant flowers.

Sometimes Pooh and Piglet would visit
their other friends together.
The two often went
to Rabbit's house
at mealtimes.

They listened to many
a family story from Owl.

They helped
Kanga with her
knitting.

And they flew kites with Christopher Robin.
Everyone knew that where there was
Pooh, there was Piglet.

One day, when the two were out walking, a bee went by. Without hesitation, Pooh and his tummy followed it.

But at the same exact time the bee flew by in one direction, a beautiful butterfly fluttered by in another. Piglet ran after the butterfly to get a closer look.

And so the best friends parted ways without even realizing it.

Through his binoculars, Piglet watched with delight as the colorful butterfly went from flower to flower. He looked closely at its lovely wings.

"Would you like to look at the butterfly with my binoculars, Pooh?" Piglet asked without looking behind him. He thought Pooh was nearby, as usual. "It's really quite a lovely creature!"

Instead of an approving snore, there was only silence. Piglet turned toward the tree where Pooh liked to nap. But there was no bear napping there. In fact, there was no bear there at all!

"Oh, d-dear!" said Piglet, alarmed. "What has happened to you, Pooh?"

Piglet wondered where Pooh had gone off to without him.
Or, rather, had Piglet been the one to go off without Pooh?

In either case, Piglet had to find his friend. He hurried off.
He wasn't sure where he was headed, but he knew he'd be
there when Pooh was there, too.

Meanwhile, Pooh had finished his encounter with the bee—or rather bees—and was having similar thoughts about Piglet.

Buzz

Buzz

Buzz

Buzzzz

Not at all sure how he had wound up without Piglet *or* honey,
Pooh resolved to find first one, then the other.

Eventually, Pooh and Piglet came across each other on a path through the Hundred-Acre Wood.

"There you are, Pooh!" cried Piglet. "But, where *were* you?"

"I'm so excited to see you again, Piglet," Pooh said. "I'm not quite sure where I was, only where I wasn't."

"I will make sure to say good-bye next time," said Piglet, smiling when he realized that there would be a next time.

"And I shall as well," Pooh said.

"It would appear that together or apart, we're still the best of friends!" said Piglet.

"Yes, that is how it would appear," Pooh agreed.

"What would you like to do tomorrow?" asked Piglet.

"Perhaps we can meet for breakfast?" said Pooh.

"Oh, that's a splendid idea," said Piglet. "And then maybe we can take a walk."

"Wonderful!" said Pooh.

Disney

Winnie the Pooh

Bounce with Me!

One day, Tigger was in a hurry to reach one of his favorite bouncing spots. He was too impatient to bounce all the way to the bridge and then bounce across it. Instead, he just bounced right over the stream!

"Hoo-hoo-hoo-hoo!" he cried. "I just invented a new game! A *superiffic* one!

Which isn't all that surprising—since inventing games is what tiggers do best!"

Tigger couldn't wait to tell his friends about his game. He **bounced** across the stream—and landed on Eeyore's house.

"Guess what?" Tigger said. "I just invented a new bouncing game. It's called, uh . . ." He paused to think.

"Take your time," Eeyore said with a sigh. "I wasn't doing anything important anyway."

"It's called bounce over the brook!" Tigger finished at last. "BOB for short."

"I'm the best BOB player ever!" Tigger went on. "Betcha can't beat me!"

"I bet you're right," Eeyore agreed gloomily. "I'm not much of a bouncer."

"Just give it a try," Tigger said. "One little bounce?"

Eeyore tried to **bounce**. But his feet hardly left the ground.

"*That's* what you call a bounce?" Tigger exclaimed. "Clearly, bouncing is NOT what eeyores do best!"

Eeyore sighed again. "Told you so."

Since Eeyore couldn't play with him, Tigger **bounced** over to Pooh's house. Pooh and Piglet were there, sharing some honey.

"Hello!" Tigger cried, **bouncing** Pooh right off his feet . . . and a honeypot right onto Piglet's head!

"Hello, Tigger," Pooh said. "Care for a smackerel of honey?"

"Tiggers do *not* like honey," Tigger said. "But they do like playing BOB."

"Bob?" Piglet said, confused. "Who's that?"

"It's not a *who*, it's a *what*. Come on! I'll show you!" Tigger **bounced** off without waiting for a reply.

71

Pooh and Piglet followed Tigger
to the stream, where Tigger explained
his new game.

"You just **bounce** over—like
this!" He demonstrated ten or eleven
times. "Give it a try, Pooh Boy!"

Pooh had never really
bounced before. But
Tigger made it look
like fun.

Pooh bent his knees. He swung his arms.
He pushed off. . . .

Splash!

Pooh sat up. He hadn't made it across the stream.
He was *in* the stream, feeling like a Soggy Bear
of Great Dampness.

"Bouncing is NOT what pooh
bears do best," Tigger declared.

Eventually, Tigger ended up at Kanga's house, hoping to find Roo. Kanga was home baking a cake.

"I'm sorry, dear, but Roo is out playing in the Wood," Kanga said kindly. "I'm not sure when he'll be back, but you can come in and help me bake my cake if you like."

Tigger was excited to help, but when he accidentally **bounced** Kanga's batter right off the table, a thought occurred to him. His bouncing was something his friends did *not* like at all.

74

Tigger left Kanga's house and **bounced** toward the stream. But his **bounces** kept getting smaller.

And smaller.

And smaller.

Finally they weren't really **bounces** at all. What was the point? None of his friends even liked his **bouncing**. It was no wonder Tigger couldn't find anyone to play BOB with him.

"A game's not much fun if you've got nobody to play with,"
Tigger muttered. "Feeling lonely is *not* what tiggers do best."

Suddenly Tigger heard laughter coming from just ahead.

"I *recognizize* that laugh," Tigger said. He bounced toward the sound and soon spotted Roo.

"Hi, Tigger!" Roo said.

"Hi, Little Buddy," Tigger said. "Want to do some bouncing? I just invented a great new game!"

Tigger and Roo bounced to the stream, and Tigger showed Roo how to play BOB.

"This is great!" Roo cried as he and Tigger bounced from one side of the stream to the other. "Look at me, Tigger.

"Whee!"

"Hoo-hoo-hoo-hoo!" Tigger cried. "Playing BOB is what tiggers *and* roos do best!"

It was true. Tigger had finally found the perfect friend to **bounce** with him!

Meanwhile, the friends met to discuss Tigger.

"I think BOB is a splendid game for Tigger," Owl began.

"It *does* keep him away from my garden," Rabbit admitted.

"I'll stay much cleaner," Piglet said brightly.

"And I'll stay much drier," added Pooh.

So it was decided . . . BOB was the perfect game for Tigger.

Tigger was having such fun that he didn't notice his friends arriving. Suddenly, he heard clapping.

"That was a fine bounce, Tigger," Pooh called out.

"Good show, little Roo," Owl added.

The rest of Tigger's friends were there as well, clapping and cheering, which made Tigger bounce higher than ever. Tigger's friends might not be very good at bouncing. But cheering on their friends? Well, that was what they ALL did best!

Disney

Winnie the Pooh

The
Pooh Sticks
Game

It had been a particularly windy night in the Hundred-Acre Wood. So windy in fact, that when Eeyore opened his eyes the next morning, he found himself looking up at the sky. The wind had toppled his house of sticks on top of him.

Eeyore had just moved all the sticks into a nice tidy pile, when Pooh and Piglet happened by on their morning walk.

"Why, Eeyore," Pooh said, "I see you've changed your house. Where, may I ask, is the front door? Or the back door, for that matter?"

"We'd be happy to help rebuild your house," said Piglet.

"Indeed we would," said Pooh. He picked up a stick.

"Those sticks don't want to stick together anymore," Eeyore said. "It's time to get new ones."

Pooh scratched his head. Suddenly the bear of little brain had a big idea.

"Eeyore," he said, "if you have no use for these sticks, I believe I know something they'd be good for. A game of Pooh Sticks!"

"Pooh Sticks!" said Piglet, clapping his hands. It had been a long time since the friends had played this game. In Pooh Sticks, several players each drop a stick over one side of the bridge and into the water. The one whose stick emerges first from under the other side of the bridge is declared the winner.

It took some doing, but Eeyore managed to make it to the bridge with the sticks. Eager to begin the game, everyone grabbed a stick and ran to one side of the bridge. They all threw their sticks in at once. Then they hurried to the other side.

The first stick floated out after a minute. The problem was that everyone was rather certain the first stick was the one they had chosen . . . until more sticks began to emerge. All the sticks looked so much alike, no one could tell *who* had won!

"It could just be me," said Eeyore, "but this game isn't as much fun as I remember."

"I think," said Christopher Robin, "that there are too many of us playing at the same time. Maybe we should take turns, like we used to."

"Take turns instead of sticks?" said Eeyore. "I don't remember doing that."

"No, no," Christopher Robin hurried to explain. "Take turns with the sticks." He looked at the sticks. They all looked the same. "We need to mark these sticks so we know whose is whose."

"I have just the thing for that!" cried Piglet, who hurried off and returned with his paints. "Everyone should paint their stick so they can recognize it. I'll paint mine yellow!"

"Splendid idea, Piglet!" said Owl, who painted his stick green like the leaves of his tree home.

Tigger painted black and orange stripes down his stick. Rabbit made his entire stick orange to resemble a carrot. Each friend painted their stick a different color.

94

Everyone gathered into groups of three. Pooh stepped up to the railing with Roo and Piglet. "Ready, set, throw!" called Rabbit.

Three sticks went into the water and floated under the bridge.

PLUNK!

PLINK!

PLONK!

After a few minutes, Pooh's red stick came out. Hooray!

Next, Kanga, Rabbit, and Owl lined up and waited for
Christopher Robin to give them the signal to drop their sticks.
Kanga dropped hers with a flick of her wrist.
Rabbit sent his down tip first, and
Owl released his as gently as
if he were shedding
a feather.

They hurried to the
other side, just in time
to see Kanga's pretty
pink stick emerge.

Everyone
cheered!

Christopher Robin, Tigger, and Eeyore
were the last three to play. "On the
count of three," said Owl.

"ONE . . .
one and a half . . .
TWO . . .
two and three eighths . . .
THREE!"

Christopher Robin let
his stick roll off his palm.

Tigger **dropped** his mid-bounce.

Eeyore did a **twitchy** move and opened his mouth to release his stick.

Eeyore's **twitchy** move worked. He won his round! "Didn't expect that," he said, with the tiniest hint of a smile.

Everyone was so excited, they couldn't wait for the final round to begin! Pooh, Kanga, and Eeyore wished each other good luck.

Piglet waved a leaf as a signal to start. PLUNK!

PLINK! PLONK!

Three Pooh Sticks went into the water and disappeared under the bridge.

100

A lone gray stick floated forward in first place. Eeyore could
hardly believe his eyes.

"Hooray for Eeyore!" everyone shouted at once. "You won!"

"Must be a mistake," said the disbelieving donkey.

"No, Eeyore." Christopher Robin laughed. "We followed
the rules and took turns. It's no mistake! You won fair
and square!"

"Taking turns?" said Eeyore. "Who knew?" Just then, he remembered that he still needed a house. He turned to go.

"Wait!" said Pooh. "We're still going to help you build your house."

Eeyore looked back. "You are?" he asked.

"We can take turns adding sticks to it," said Roo excitedly.

"Because that's what friends do!" said Christopher Robin.

Disney
Winnie the Pooh

Don't Be Roo-diculous!

One sunny afternoon, Roo and Tigger were **bouncing** together in the Hundred-Acre Wood.

Roo looked up at a nearby tree. "Let's see who can reach that branch first!" he cried.

"You got it, Little Buddy!" said Tigger.

Roo jumped up, up, up. But he still couldn't come anywhere near the tree branch. Tigger touched it easily. When Roo came down, he lost his balance. . .

. . . and landed in a bed of flowers.

"Picking some flowers for your mama?" asked Tigger.

"I guess," said Roo sadly.

"What's the matter, Little Buddy?" asked Tigger.

"I wish I could bounce as high as you," said Roo.

"Don't be *roo-diculous*," said Tigger. "You **bounce** pretty good for a little fella."

Tigger picked some flowers and handed them to Roo. "Besides," he added as he **bounced** off, "bouncing is what tiggers do best!"

107

Roo sighed into the flowers. "I wish I weren't so small," he said. He looked up at the tree. "One day," he said out loud, "I want to reach that branch and swing from it!"

"Pardon me for interrupting, but perhaps I can help," said Winnie the Pooh, who was on his way back from Piglet's house.

"Do you really think so, Pooh?" asked Roo, looking at his friend with interest. Perhaps, he thought, Pooh really did know something about how to be **bigger**.

"Why, yes," said Pooh. He took the flowers out of Roo's arms and lifted up his little friend. Pooh carried Roo until they were underneath the tree branch in question. Then he held Roo up. Pooh had to stand on his tippytoes, and Roo had to s-t-r-e-t-c-h his arms as high as they would go . . . but it worked! Roo was able to reach the tree branch!

"Whee!" cried Roo, as he swung from the branch. "I'll rest here while you play, and make sure you get down safely. Just let me know when you're ready," said Pooh.

No sooner had Pooh's back touched the tree than he fell asleep. Roo swung happily for a few minutes. Then his arms got tired. "Oh, Pooh?" he called down.

Z Z Z Z Z Z was Pooh's response.

Roo didn't want to wake Pooh, so he scrambled up onto the branch. Now he could swing his legs, which was much easier than swinging by his arms. Even so, Roo began to grow bored. If I were **bigger**, he thought, I could get down by myself!

After what seemed like a long time to Roo,
he heard someone coming. It was Christopher Robin.

Not terribly surprised to find Pooh snoozing against a tree,
Christopher Robin *was* very surprised to find Roo sitting *in* the
tree. Roo explained what had happened.

"I can help you down," said Christopher Robin, who didn't want to wake Pooh either. He held out his arms, and Roo jumped safely into them.

Once back on the ground, Roo thanked Christopher Robin. Then he scooped up the flowers and unhappily headed home.

The next day, Roo went off to have a good, long sulk. He wasn't sure why, but sulking reminded him of Eeyore. And without really planning it, Roo wound up at his friend's house of sticks.

Eeyore wasn't home, so Roo sat down to wait for him to return. Absentmindedly, he picked up a stick that had fallen from Eeyore's house. As Roo examined it, he began thinking it would be useful for lots of things besides Eeyore's house—a Pooh Sticks stick, a pretend sword . . .

Suddenly, Roo had an idea. "That's it!" he cried. "I know just what to do." And he hurried off.

Roo stopped by Rabbit's house and

borrowed a hammer and nails. Then he went into

the woods and collected as many sticks as he could find.

Roo began to nail sticks to a very TALL tree. Before long,

he had a ladder that he could climb to reach the tree branches

without anyone's help!

Roo couldn't help but feel rather proud of himself. He resolved to make ladders on several more trees. But for now, he climbed the tree in front of him and happily swung from its branches.

Roo was unaware of how much time had passed, until he
heard his mother's worried cry: "Roo!"

Then he heard Rabbit, Owl,

Tigger, and Pooh calling him, too.

"I'm up here!" he shouted.

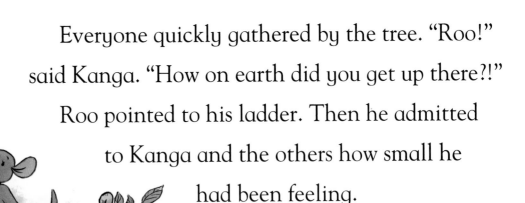

Everyone quickly gathered by the tree. "Roo!"
said Kanga. "How on earth did you get up there?!"
Roo pointed to his ladder. Then he admitted
to Kanga and the others how small he
had been feeling.

"That's using your noggin!" said Tigger, admiring the ladder. "There's nothing small about your brain, Little Buddy!"

Roo grinned from ear to ear as he climbed down.

121

"I'm so proud of you, dear," Kanga said. "You didn't give up. You kept at it until you figured out how to feel bigger!

"And don't worry," she added. "You will be bigger soon enough." Kanga lifted a tired little Roo into her pouch. "But for now, you're just the right size!"

DISNEY
Winnie the Pooh
Friendly Bothers

Rabbit liked to keep things neat and tidy. His house was neat and tidy.

His larder was neat and tidy.

His garden was neat and tidy.

There was just one problem: Rabbit's *friends* weren't all neat and tidy. Especially certain friends.

"Howdy, Ol' Long Ears!" Tigger cried, scattering rakes, watering cans, and turnips every which way.

"Isn't it a *stupenderous* day for bouncing?"

Then Rabbit turned to see Pooh digging up the spot where he'd just planted his turnips. "What are you doing?" he cried.

"I dug a hole so you can plant your turnips again where Tigger bounced them," Pooh explained helpfully.

"Noooo!" Rabbit screeched. "Must you two make a mess everywhere you go? Get out! Get out now!"

"What are you tryin' to say, Long Ears?" Tigger said.

"GET OUT!" Rabbit howled at the top of his lungs.

Pooh and Tigger turned to go.

"Sorry, Rabbit," Pooh called over his shoulder.

Rabbit had just started collecting the scattered honeypots when he heard someone coming. "I said get out!" he shouted.

Then he turned and saw that it was Kanga and Roo.

"Er, sorry about the shouting," he told them. "I thought you were someone else."

"Who'd you think we were, Rabbit?" Roo asked curiously. "And why'd you tell 'em to get out?"

"I thought you were Tigger and Pooh." Rabbit frowned as he thought about the pair. "They've been messing up my place all day long! I can't take it anymore!"

Little Roo looked sad. "Does that mean Tigger and Pooh aren't your friends anymore?" he asked.

Rabbit shrugged. "Never thought of it that way."

"But you told them to get out and not come back," Roo said. "That doesn't sound very friendly." He sighed. "I'd sure miss Tigger and Pooh if they weren't *my* friends anymore."

"I would too, dear," Kanga said. "Pooh has the warmest heart in the Hundred-Acre Wood. His visits always make me happy."

Roo nodded. "And Tigger's lots of fun! He never gets tired of playing, and he always lets me pick the game."

"I think you could be a little more patient with your friends," Kanga told Rabbit kindly.

"Bah!" Rabbit said. "I don't know how to be *that* patient!"

"All good gardeners know how to be patient," Kanga said.

"Hmm. You're right about that." Rabbit looked around his tidy garden. "Gardening's hard work, and it takes time." He frowned. "That's why it's so infuriating when Tigger bounces through and wrecks the place!"

"But you don't get upset with the wind when it blows leaves into your garden, do you?" Kanga inquired.

Rabbit shook his head. "A blustery day *can* make a mess. But the wind helps spread seeds and pollen."

"Do you get mad when your garden needs water?" she asked.

"Don't be silly!" Rabbit said. "Every garden needs water to grow. I give my garden as much water as it needs, even if it means filling the watering can twenty times."

"See?" Roo clapped his hands. "You *are* patient, Rabbit!"

Rabbit wasn't sure what to think. "Well, maybe I am."

The following day, Tigger and Pooh paid Rabbit another visit.

"Are you still upset with us, Rabbit?" Pooh asked.

Before Rabbit could answer, a gust of wind grabbed his hat and blew it up into a tall tree.

"Drat, my hat!" Rabbit cried.

"Leave it to me," Tigger said. "I'll get it back for ya!"

He bounced wa-a-a-ay up into the tree and grabbed the hat, then landed again—right in Rabbit's pumpkin patch! For a moment Rabbit saw red.

But the wind reminded him of what Kanga had said. Tigger made a mess sometimes, just like the wind. But he was only trying to help.

"Thank you, Tigger," Rabbit said as patiently as he could. "Your bouncing *does* come in handy now and then."

Thud!

"Shall I help pick up these honeypots, Rabbit?" Pooh offered.
"I could even double-check to make sure there's no honey left
in them."

He reached for a honeypot. But he accidentally knocked over
Rabbit's watering can.

"Oh, no!" Rabbit cried.

But the water made him remember Kanga's words again. Pooh needed a lot of honey to keep his tummy happy, just like Rabbit's garden needed a lot of water to make it grow. And now that Rabbit thought about it, a few smackerels of honey were a small price to pay for Pooh's cheerful visits.

"Thank you, Pooh," he said patiently. "I was about to water that part of the garden anyway."

From then on, Rabbit still tried to keep things neat and tidy. But it didn't bother him as much when Pooh ate all his honey. And he didn't get quite as aggravated when Tigger was a little too bouncy.

Instead, he tried to be patient and look for the good things in Pooh, Tigger, and all of his other friends in the Wood.

After all, that was what friends were for.

Disney

Winnie the Pooh

Better Than Honey?

"Good morning, Rabbit," Pooh said politely one day. "Have you had breakfast yet?"

Rabbit looked suspicious. "Yes," he said. "Haven't you?"

"Why, no, I haven't. Thank you for inviting me," Pooh said.

"Did I?" Rabbit looked rather confused. "Well, then I suppose you'd better come in."

Soon, Pooh was enjoying a smackerel of honey. "I never tasted such delicious honey," he said in a sticky voice.

"I never knew someone so obsessed with honey." Rabbit sounded a bit cross. "Don't you ever do anything but eat honey, Pooh Bear?"

Pooh stopped eating. "I suppose I must do other things sometimes, mustn't I?" Pooh said. "The trouble is, I can't quite think of what those things might be just now."

"Well, there's no more honey," Rabbit said.

"Oh, dear," Pooh said. "Well, what are you going to do now, Rabbit? Because perhaps I could do the same thing."

"I'm going to work in my garden," Rabbit answered.

Pooh didn't know much about gardening. But he agreed to give it a try. First he helped Rabbit pick some carrots.

Then they watered the peas.

After that, it was time to mulch the tomatoes.

Pooh enjoyed all of it. It wasn't the same as eating honey. But it was fun to try something different.

"That's enough gardening, Pooh," Rabbit said after a while. "Why don't you go find something else to do?"

"Like eating honey?" Pooh said hopefully. "Is there any more?"

"No," Rabbit replied. "You'll have to think of something else."

Pooh wandered off, thinking as hard as he could. Then he noticed that he was near Owl's house.

Owl is the wisest friend I have, Pooh said to himself. Perhaps he'll be able to help me figure out what to do now.

149

Owl listened to Pooh's dilemma. "This puts me in mind of my great-aunt Phyllis," he said. "She loved trying new things. Knitting, baking, checkers, camel racing, fly-tying . . ."

Owl went on and on and on. Pooh tried to keep up with what he was saying, but the words piled up far too quickly.

Finally Owl stopped talking. "So, which of those interesting things would you suggest I try, Owl?" Pooh asked politely.

Owl peered at him in surprise. "Weren't you listening, Pooh?" he asked. "Aunt Phyllis told me she was never so happy as when she was writing her memoirs. You ought to do that."

After thinking about his memoirs, Pooh's tummy **rumbled**. "Is it lunchtime already?" he asked Eeyore, who was walking by.

He thought about stopping by Rabbit's house for some tasty honey. But thinking about Rabbit reminded Pooh that he was supposed to be trying new things today.

"May I join you, Eeyore?" he asked. "Eating thistles for lunch sounds like a delicious new thing to try."

"It does?" Eeyore said doubtfully.

"Well?" Eeyore asked Pooh. "How do you like the thistles?"

"They're, er, different," Pooh said politely, picking a prickly bit of thistle out of his tongue. "They'd probably be even tastier with a smackerel of honey."

Next, Pooh and Tigger **bounced** together for a while.

"Whaddaya think, Pooh Boy?" Tigger said.

"It's very interesting," Pooh replied breathlessly, "but rather tiring. And it does make one a bit hungry."

Next, Pooh found Roo and they played together in the sand
until Kanga appeared. "Bath time, Roo," she said.

"Aw, do I have to, Mama?" Roo asked.

"Bath time sounds interesting," Pooh said. "Can I try it, too?"

Kanga sized him up uncertainly. "I'm not sure you

and the water will both fit in
the tub, Pooh," she said. "But
if you want something to do,
you could wash the soup pot
for me."

"All right," Pooh said.

"That sounds interesting, too."

It turned out that Kanga knew about lots
of interesting new things Pooh could try,

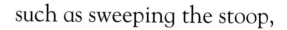

such as sweeping the stoop,

stirring the porridge,

carrying in some apples for supper, and much more.

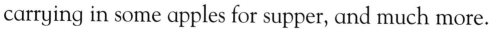

Pooh was hanging the laundry out to dry when
Christopher Robin appeared. "Hello, Pooh Bear," the boy
said. "What have you been up to today?"

"Oh, all sorts of things." Pooh told Christopher Robin
about his day. "Some things I tried made me
more hungry, and some made me less hungry."
Pooh sighed. "But I'm afraid all of them
made me think about honey."

Christopher Robin laughed. "Silly old bear," he said. "Of course they did! Pooh Bears are meant to eat honey."

Pooh felt confused. "So I shouldn't try new things after all?"

"No, it's good to try new things," the boy said. "Otherwise, how would you know how much you liked your old things?"

"Shall we go find some honey then?" Pooh asked.

"That sounds like the best idea you've had all day," Christopher Robin agreed.

Disney
Winnie the Pooh
Forget Me Knot

Winnie the Pooh hurried to the breakfast table. He did this every morning, but today he was excited not only about breakfast, but about the whole day ahead. He knew something special was going to happen. That's why he had tied a ribbon around his favorite honeypot—so he wouldn't forget. But now he couldn't remember what the something special was.

Before Pooh had been outside for very long, Piglet came whistling down the walk. Now, seeing Piglet was always something special. But, somehow, Pooh was rather certain that today's something special was something else.

Piglet stayed for a visit. "I don't remember
when I've had such a good time, Piglet," said Pooh.
"Except for the last time we were together. And then
there was the last time I saw Christopher Robin."

"Christopher Robin!" cried Pooh, sitting up. "That's the something special that's supposed to happen today! Christopher Robin is coming to visit me."

"What time is he coming?" asked Piglet.

"Umpteen o'clock, I believe," said Pooh, a bit uncertainly. "Is it umpteen o'clock yet, Piglet?"

165

"I'm pretty sure umpteen o'clock has come and gone, Pooh," said Piglet.

Pooh suddenly looked very sad. "There, there, Pooh," said Piglet."

"Christopher Robin was late once before," said Piglet. "Don't you remember? He was late because he was bringing you some honeypots. He had so many, it slowed him down.

"That's just the kind of friend he is," Piglet added.

The next one to come by, however, was Rabbit, wheeling a cart loaded with rutabagas. "Would you like some, Pooh?" asked Rabbit. "I always grow more than I can eat. And when I think of someone able to eat more than I grow, I think of you."

"That's very kind of you, Rabbit," said Pooh, who then inquired about Christopher Robin.

"Well, he's probably just been delayed," said Rabbit. "If he weren't coming, he'd have sent you some sort of word. You know how he is. He's very loyal. I remember the time you thought you'd lost your favorite honeypot." Rabbit gestured to the one on the ground. "That one, there."

"Don't you remember how Christopher Robin wouldn't go home until he helped you find it?" said Rabbit.

"Yes," said Pooh, remembering. "It turned out I had left it under a hive, hoping the bees would fill it back up with honey."

Rabbit went off with his vegetables, and a few minutes later Tigger came bouncing by.

"Whatcha doin', Pooh Boy?" asked Tigger.

Pooh explained that he was waiting for Christopher Robin.

"Oooooh," Tigger said, when Pooh had finished. "If it's Christopher Robin you want, it's Christopher Robin you'll get. Wait here, Pooh Boy. I'll go find him."

Tigger was gone for just a few minutes. But, when he came **bouncing** back, he didn't have Christopher Robin with him. He had Eeyore.

"That Christopher Robin is nowhere to be found," said Tigger. "But I'm sure this is just some minor *mixer-uperoo*. So I brought you Donkey Boy instead." And off Tigger **bounced**.

Eeyore sat down next to Pooh, and the two spent the rest of the day in companionable silence, until the sun set behind the trees.

Eeyore got up to go. "Sorry he didn't make it," he said as he started to leave.

Then Eeyore turned and looked back at Pooh. "Don't worry," he said. "That boy is a better friend to you than my tail is to me. You can't get rid of him so easily."

"Thank you, Eeyore," said Pooh. "You're quite right, I'm sure."

Pooh knew that Christopher Robin was a friend he could trust. That was why he found what had happened—or rather what hadn't happened—so odd. For the rest of the evening Pooh wondered and worried about Christopher Robin.

Pooh slept fitfully that night. He tossed and turned and dreamed that his pillow was a marshmallow. He woke up when he tried to eat it.

Pooh realized that it was morning. And that someone was gently pulling the pillow out of his mouth. It was Christopher Robin! The something special had finally arrived, and that was a wonderful surprise.

"Pooh," said Christopher Robin, "I know I'm early, but I just couldn't wait to spend the day with you today."

"Today?" asked Pooh. "Not umpteen o'clock yesterday?"

"Pooh," said Christopher Robin, "did you forget the date and the time again?"

"Do I do that?" said Pooh.

"All the time," said Christopher Robin.

"It would appear that I forgot that I forget," Pooh said.

Christopher Robin took the ribbon and knotted it around Pooh's favorite honeypot once again.

"Silly old bear," he said. "You're likely to mix up the details again. So, let this ribbon remind you that you can count on me, no matter what."

"*That* I shall never forget," said Pooh.

Disney

Winnie the Pooh

Owl's Reading Lessons

Everyone knew that Owl was the best reader in the Hundred-Acre Wood. Whenever his friends wanted to hear a story, Owl selected a book to read aloud to them. One particularly fine spring day found him doing just that. " '. . . and the goat became the best clockmaker in town and lived happily ever after,' " Owl read. " 'The end.' "

Owl closed the book.

"Read us another one, Owl!" Roo begged. "Please?"

Owl cleared his throat. "Perhaps later," he said. "I should rest my voice for a bit. My birthday is tomorrow, you see, and I suspect I may be called upon to make a speech for the occasion." He went to return the book to his library.

"Oh, dear," said Piglet. "I hope Owl doesn't mind reading to us so often."

Piglet turned to look at Pooh, who hadn't said a word. "What do you think, Pooh Bear?"

Pooh was thinking, an activity that didn't come easily for a bear of very little brain.

But this time, Pooh's little brain had a big idea.

"Perhaps Owl would like it," Pooh said carefully, "if *we* read to *him* once in a while. Perhaps on his birthday."

185

The friends were too excited to wait for Owl's return, so they hurried over and knocked on his door.

"Owl, may I borrow a book?" Pooh asked politely when Owl answered the door.

"May you *what* a *who*?" Owl said in surprise.

"Borrow a book," Pooh repeated. "If you happen to have one to spare."

Owl couldn't remember the last time one of his friends had asked to borrow a book. In fact, he was fairly certain that none of his friends had *ever* asked to borrow a book.

"Er, of course," he said. "Which book would you like?"

"I'm not sure," Pooh admitted. "I thought I'd just try a little reading."

"Me, too," Piglet added.

"And us, too," said Tigger, Rabbit, and Roo.

Eeyore sighed. "I s'pose I'll give it a try."

So Owl helped each of his friends select books. For Pooh, he found a book all about how bees make honey.

For Roo, there was an exciting storybook with lots of pictures. "Hooray!" Roo cheered.

Rabbit spotted a **big** book about vegetables. "This one looks interesting," he said.

189

"Here's one for you, Tigger," Owl said. "There's not much **bouncing** in it, but I think you'll like it nonetheless."

"Don't worry, Eeyore. I haven't forgotten you," Owl said.

"It's all right. I'm not very memorable," Eeyore said.

Owl pulled out a book filled with cheerful pictures of rainbows and blue skies. "This book is sure to make you feel jolly," he told Eeyore.

Soon, Pooh had settled down at his Thoughtful Spot for a good read. He opened his book to the first page. It had several rather long and alarming-looking words on it, along with a picture of a beehive full of delicious-looking honey.

Pooh's tummy let out a rumble. "Well, no sense trying to read on an empty stomach," he said.

Tucking his book under one arm, Pooh set off for home.

All around the Wood, the others were working
on their reading, too.

Tigger read the entire first letter of
his book. . . .

Then he decided to
celebrate by bouncing
for a while.

Rabbit enjoyed his book about vegetables very much. "That
reminds me," he muttered as he came upon a picture of a
rutabaga. "I've been meaning to reorganize my larder all week.
No time like the present!"

The next morning Pooh awoke thinking of honey. He used a book to reach a honeypot on his top shelf.

"Oh, bother," he said, looking at the book. "I forgot to learn to read."

At that very moment, Tigger was realizing the same thing. "I guess reading's not what tiggers do best after all," he said sadly.

"Mama!" Roo cried when he woke up. "I didn't learn Owl's story yet!"

Eeyore felt gloomy as usual when he opened his eyes. "Knew I forgot something important. Then again, I usually do."

"Drat," Rabbit said when he noticed the book by his neatly organized larder. "Is Owl's birthday here already?"

195

The friends all gathered at Owl's house. "Happy birthday, Owl," Pooh said sadly. "We're sorry."

"Yes, terribly sorry," Rabbit added.

"Whatever do you mean?" Owl asked. "Sorry for what?"

Pooh held up his book. "Each of us wanted to read you a story for your birthday," he explained.

"But we couldn't figger out all the words," Tigger added.

Roo nodded. "There are an awful lot of words."

"Sorry, Owl," Piglet finished.

"Are you terribly disappointed, Owl?" Pooh asked.

To everyone's surprise, Owl smiled. He'd been afraid his friends had grown tired of listening to him read. But they were just trying to do something thoughtful.

"I'm not disappointed," he said. "It's the thought that counts."

Piglet still looked worried. "But if there's to be any reading today, you'll have to do it yourself," he pointed out.

"Then it's a good thing I saved my voice yesterday, eh?" Owl said happily. "Because it seems I have a good bit of reading to do today. Now, where shall we start?"

"Happy birthday, Owl!" Roo cheered. "Read mine first!"

Owl took Roo's book. Then he cleared his throat and began. "'Once upon a time, there lived a brave and noble knight. . . .'"

Owl read that book, and all the others, aloud to his friends. And in the end, everyone decided it had been one of the best, and most educational, birthdays any of them could ever remember.

Disney
Winnie the Pooh
Under-the-Weather Friends

ACHOO!

It was a beautiful day outside in the Hundred-Acre Wood. But Winnie the Pooh was inside. Not only was he inside, he was in bed. What had started out as a case of the sniffles had blossomed into a full-blown cold.

Pooh's ears were a bit clogged, so he sneezed as loud as he could so he could hear himself.

ACHOO!!

Piglet followed the sneezing sounds all the way through the Wood. When he arrived at Pooh's front door, he realized that it wasn't just anybody sneezing. It was Pooh!

ACHOO!! ACHOO!! Pooh had to close his eyes every time he sneezed.

It was after one such series of sneezes that Pooh opened his eyes to find Piglet, along with their other friends.

"Good morning, dear," said Kanga. "Piglet told us you're under the weather. We've come to take care of you."

Pooh couldn't believe his good fortune to have so many kind and helpful friends.

Everyone got to work immediately. Kanga went into Pooh's kitchen to heat up a fresh batch of soup. Rabbit went with her to help her find just the right pot.

Clang! Bang! Looking for the right soup pot was very noisy when it was Rabbit doing the looking. And he and Kanga could not agree on which was the proper pot for warming soup, nor on the proper soup to serve for a cold. Their loud voices carried their points of view into Pooh's bedroom.

Although Pooh's ears were clogged, Rabbit and even gentle Kanga still seemed rather loud. And to make matters even noisier, Owl, who had positioned himself in a chair right next to Pooh's bed, was reading to him from a volume of Owl's family history.

Owl was straining to be heard over Piglet, who was speaking to Pooh.

Poor Pooh's headache was only getting worse. ACHOO!!

Knock   Knock   Knock   Knock   Knock

The sound of all his friends trying to make him feel better was making Pooh feel worse. And his head felt as if someone was knocking on it.

The knocking turned out to be Christopher Robin, who had also come to help take care of his favorite bear.

Christopher Robin took a look around. Then he clapped his hands. Everyone stopped what they were doing and gathered around the boy.

"I'm happy to see that Pooh has so many wonderful friends," Christopher Robin said. He glanced at Pooh. Pooh nodded his head and smiled. And sneezed.

"But, perhaps," the boy said carefully, "you might each take a turn doing something for Pooh—so as not to tire him out, that is."

Everyone thought that made sense. First, Roo sang Pooh a "Get Well" song.

Eeyore gathered some daises and put them in a vase. Piglet began to sweep.

Rabbit agreed to let Kanga serve the soup. "But," he said, "it will taste better with a slice of carrot bread. I'll bake some now!"

213

ACHOO!! ACHOO!! Suddenly Piglet gave two
extra-loud sneezes that startled everyone, including himself.
"It must be the dust from my sweeping," he said.

The food, the tidy house, and, most of all, his friends
made Pooh feel much better by the end of the afternoon.

Kanga plumped Pooh's pillows
as the friends prepared to
leave for the day.

ACHOO!!

ACHOO!!

"We'll be back tomorrow
to check on you, Pooh!" said
Piglet, who was still a bit sneezy.

Pooh nodded, drowsy and content. "It's lovely how you all fuss over me." He sighed happily.

"It's what friends do, Pooh Boy!" said Tigger as he **bounced** off.

"Of course it is," said Rabbit, who tugged on Pooh's covers, smoothing them out before he left with the others.

217

The next day, Pooh was feeling much better. When his friends
came to check on him, they found him dressed and outside,
breathing in the fresh air.

"It seems that your cold has gone away, Pooh!" said Owl.

"So it does," said Pooh.

ACHOO!! ACHOO!! The sound of sneezing came through the Hundred-Acre Wood. Everyone looked at each other, confused. Then they realized that Piglet was missing, and that the sneezing was coming from the direction of his house.

"Oh, dear," said Pooh. "It would appear that my cold has gone away, but not very far."

"Well," said Kanga, "now we know just what to do."

"We can all take turns making Piglet feel better!" Roo cried.

"'Cuz takin' turns is what friends do best!" Tigger said.

"Hoo-hoo-hoo-hoo!"

DISNEY
Winnie the Pooh

A Bounciful
Friendship

Tigger was having a *bounciful* day in the Hundred-Acre Wood.
He bounced this way.

He bounced that way.

He bounced this way again. And then he decided to bounce over to Winnie the Pooh's house.

Pooh was cleaning out his cupboards and carrying his honeypots outside. As he was placing a honeypot on the ground, Tigger **bounced** straight into him.

"Oh, bother," said Pooh.

Tigger looked at the mess. "That's quite a lot of sticky grass you've got there, Pooh Boy," he said, whistling at the sight of it all.

Pooh began to put honey back into the pots.

"Would you like some help?" asked Tigger. "Getting out of sticky situations is what tiggers do best!"

"No, but thank you all the same, Tigger," said Pooh.

"Well, seeing as you have your hands full, I'll go see what our pal Piglet is up to. T-T-F-N!" cried Tigger, bouncing off.

"Hallooo, Pigalet!" shouted Tigger, bouncing into Piglet. "Whatcha up to?"

Piglet got up rather slowly, making sure that nothing in his little body had been broken by Tigger's big greeting.

"I was collecting haycorns," said Piglet, holding

out his empty basket.

Tigger looked in Piglet's basket. "Sure you were, little buddy,"

he said, trying to be supportive. "Them *invisimible* ones are my

favorite kind!"

Tigger decided to **bounce on over** to Rabbit's next. As usual, Rabbit was busy in his garden.

Tigger didn't notice the rake right in front of him—until he **bounced** on it and fell on top of Rabbit's plants!

"You're **crushing** my rutabagas!" Rabbit shouted.

CRUNCH!

"Why don't you go and **bounce** somewhere else?"

"Hallooo, Eeyore!" cried Tigger, bouncing in so suddenly and loudly that Eeyore fell into the side of his house.

Crack! Crash! Twigs came tumbling down.

Tigger helped Eeyore up and brushed him off. "I sure didn't expect *that* to happen," said Tigger.

"Neither did I," said Eeyore.

"Tigger, your bouncing is out of control!" called Rabbit, walking up. Pooh, Piglet, and the others were behind him.

"But tiggers are bounciful when they're happy." Tigger said.

Rabbit and everyone else knew that was true. But Rabbit was still annoyed. "You need to be a little *less* happy and a lot more respectful of others and their things!" he declared.

"That is, if you wouldn't mind," added Pooh. Piglet nodded.

Tigger looked around at all his friends. He looked at the ruins of Eeyore's house. The idea that his bouncing could make his friends unhappy was something Tigger couldn't understand. Not sure what else he could say, he turned and walked away so he could think.

Christopher Robin, who was on his way to visit everyone, came across Tigger sitting with his head in his hands.

"Whatever is the matter, Tigger?" said Christopher Robin. "You seem to have lost your bounce."

Tigger told the boy about all the things he had ruined in just one day. "I don't have an ounce of bounce left," Tigger said sadly. "I'm not sure I have any friends left either."

"Why, you don't really believe that, do you, Tigger?" asked Christopher Robin.

"I'm afraid so," said Tigger with a sigh.

"Let's go find the others," said Christopher Robin kindly. "I'm sure you can mend whatever needs mending."

Suddenly Tigger **bounced up!**

"Christopher Robin, you are a genuine *gee-nee-us!* I'm going to mend *everything!*" he shouted.

"Hoo-hoo-hoo-hoo!" Tigger cried as he **bounced** off.

First, Tigger brought
Pooh new honeypots
brimming
with
honey.

Next, he planted some seeds in
Rabbit's garden.

Then he **bounced** over
to Piglet's house and filled an
entire basket of haycorns
for his friend.

And he rebuilt Eeyore's house all by himself.

"Well done, Tigger!" Christopher Robin said with pride.

"I must say I *am* feelin' pretty tiggeriffic!" said Tigger.

"Why aren't you bouncing then?" Christopher Robin asked.

"You *want* me to bounce?" asked Tigger.

"Wouldn't be you if you didn't," Eeyore said.

And so he bounced—because it turns out that bouncing *and* respecting their friends is what tiggers do best!

Disney

Winnie the Pooh

Owl Be Seeing You

The Hundred-Acre Wood was abuzz with more than bees. Winnie the Pooh and his friends had each received a formal invitation to Owl's house. It read:

COME FOR TEA AND ANOUNCEMINT OF GREAT IMPORTENS.

"An 'ounce mint'?" said Pooh, who enjoyed all sorts of sweet treats. "Why, that's very kind of Owl. Do you suppose that is a very **large** mint? And will there be one for each of us?"

Christopher Robin chuckled. "Silly old bear," he said. "I think this means that Owl has something to tell us. He's going to make an announcement."

"I see," said Pooh, but he wasn't quite sure that he did.

When the friends arrived, Owl went on and on about an upcoming family reunion until finally Rabbit stood up. "Owl!" he said. "We know all about your reunion planning. Every last little detail. But what did you want to tell us? Why are we here?"

Owl stopped speaking for a moment. "Why, indeed?" he mumbled. "Oh, yes, I know," he said. "The reunion planning is all done. It begins tomorrow. I simply wanted to share the news with you—that I shall be gone for one week!"

"Don't worry about us. We'll be just fine while you're gone," Rabbit assured Owl as he and the others said their good-byes. As soon as Owl shut his door, Rabbit clapped his hands together with glee.

"Don't you see?" exclaimed Rabbit. "We don't have to hear any more long-winded stories about Aunt Snowy or Third Cousin Barney, Twice Removed! In fact, we don't have to hear anything from Owl at all for a whole week!"

While Owl was away, things went on as usual in the Hundred-Acre Wood. Rabbit tended his garden, only without Owl looking over his shoulder and talking nonstop about the glorious gardens his grandmother had when he was a young owlet.

KERITS

Piglet painted his pictures,
but he didn't have Owl peering
at each canvas and
remarking on each
painting.

Pooh still enjoyed plenty of honey, but didn't have to listen to
Owl lecture him about the benefits of doing his stoutness
exercises—something
Owl had read
about extensively.

It was also quiet over at Kanga and Roo's house. Kanga was able to bake without Owl describing what a wonderful cook his great aunt Gladys had been.

Roo and Tigger continued to play together, but without having to stop to listen to Owl explain the science behind bouncing and other important concepts.

And Eeyore managed to rebuild his house—again—but without Owl boasting about the grand homes some of his relatives lived in.

One day, after nearly a week had gone by, Rabbit was in his garden. He had begun to feel a little lonely while working in it. Just then, two pesky crows swooped in and began to peck at his plants. They had arrived the day Owl had left, and now they bothered Rabbit every morning. "Shoo! Shoo!" Rabbit cried.

After he managed to wave the crows off, Rabbit thought for a moment. Perhaps, when Owl was around, it was too noisy for the crows. "Well," Rabbit said aloud to himself, "imagine that!"

Kanga was finding her housework was taking longer and was much more dull without Owl's company.

And now that Roo and Tigger could bounce to their hearts' content without Owl's lectures interrupting them . . . Roo realized that he got tired long before Tigger did.

"Don't worry," said Tigger. "Bouncing is what tiggers do best."
But the friends just weren't having as much fun as before.

Eeyore rebuilt his house, but he missed having Owl around.
"Seems like more work without the words," he said with a sigh.

The friends all gathered at Owl's house.

"Has Owl been gone a week yet?" asked Pooh.

"Why, it's more than that, I'm sure of it," declared Rabbit. He thought for a minute. "What if Owl decides he'd rather live with his relatives and never comes back?"

"That's *impossibabble!*" said Tigger.

"Isn't it?" Tigger looked around to see a bunch of uncertain, unhappy faces.

Suddenly the Hundred-Acre Wood was quieter than ever. Everyone was thinking the same thing: Owl could be annoying at times, but having no Owl at all was completely unacceptable.

Just then, Christopher Robin came down the path leading to Owl's house. He was pulling his red wagon, which was piled high with gifts. And walking beside Christopher Robin, talking up a storm, was none other than Owl himself!

"We thought you might have enjoyed your reunion so much that you wouldn't come back," said Pooh.

Owl shook his head. "Oh, it was a splendid reunion," he said. "But, stay with my family? Never! They talk far too much!"

"Welcome home, Owl," said Rabbit happily. "Now, tell us all about your trip!"

Disney
Winnie the Pooh
Piglet the Brave

Thud!

Piglet was **frightened** by many things. **Dark** and **spooky** shadows.

Thud!

Startling surprises.

Loud and ANGRY thunderstorms.

CRASH!

BOOM!

BOOM!

Being **all** alone.

Sometimes Piglet even felt frightened in his own cozy bed. One **dark** night, he had an especially **scary** dream. In the dream, he was collecting haycorns. All of a sudden, a haycorn fell on his head. Piglet **jumped**.

"**Oh!** You startled me!" he cried.

"How could you be scared of a tiny haycorn like me?" the haycorn asked.

Now Piglet was even more surprised. "I didn't think haycorns could talk!" he exclaimed.

"Of course we can!" a much louder voice said.

Suddenly Piglet was surrounded by giant haycorns!

"We're going to get you, tiny Piglet!" one of the giant haycorns growled.

"Nooooo!" Piglet cried. He began to run. The haycorns chased him all through the Wood. Just as Piglet thought he had managed to escape them . . .

"Aaaaaaaah!" Piglet screamed in terror, waking himself up from his terrifying dream.

When Pooh came to visit the next moring, Piglet asked, "How do you make yourself feel better after a scary dream?"

Pooh scratched his head. "I don't know," he said. "I suppose I just don't think about it."

"Oh! I'll try that then." Piglet tried NOT to think about his dream. But the more he tried NOT to think about it, the more he DID think about it!

"Oh, dear," Piglet said. "It's not working."

"What's not working?" Pooh asked.

"Not thinking about my scary dream," Piglet said.

"Oh, that. I'd already stopped thinking about it." Pooh licked some honey off his paw. "Perhaps we should ask Kanga. She tends to know a great deal about this sort of thing."

The two friends didn't find Kanga, but they did find Roo.
"I used to be afraid of shadows, too," Roo said. "But Mama told
me to use my imagination to change them from something
scary into something fun by playing make-believe! I'll show
you!" Roo offered.

He led Piglet and Pooh into the Wood. The shadows were as **dark** and **spooky** as ever. "Now what?" asked Pooh.

"Now I pretend that the shadows are something else." Roo thought for a second. "I know! I'm gonna pretend that shadow there is a kite!"

Suddenly, a giant monster leaped into view.

"Hallooo, Pigalet!" the monster exclaimed. Only it wasn't a monster at all. It was Tigger.

"Tigger!" Piglet said. "You f-f-f-frightened me!"

"Sorry about that, Piglet Ol' Pal." Tigger said. "I'd better un-frighten you, then!"

"What was it that was so frightening *exac-ta-ly*?" Tigger asked. "Was it my stripes? My whiskers? My *grr*?" He let out a **loud GRRR!** "It was probably my *grr*, wasn't it?"

"No," Piglet said. "I mean, your *grr* is quite impressive, Tigger. But what scared me was the surprise."

"I see," Tigger said. "Well, there's one way to fix that."

"By not surprising me anymore?" Piglet asked.

"Nope!" Tigger shook his head. "By surprising you MORE!"

Piglet was confused. "How will that help me be less scared?"

"You'll see. Now take a walk through the Wood, and I'll start surprisin' ya!"

272

Piglet, Pooh, and Roo started walking. Tigger disappeared.
A moment later, he **bounced** Piglet off his feet again.

"Surprise!" he cried. "Are you scared?"

Piglet smiled. "No. You told me you were going to surprise me,
so I wasn't scared at all." He gasped. "Oh! It worked!"

"Told ya so," Tigger said proudly.

Piglet got up and brushed himself off.

But, when he looked around, he realized he'd been left behind.

"Oh, d-d-dear," he murmured.

He began to run after the others, but he froze with fear when he heard footsteps behind him.

When he saw that the footsteps belonged to Eeyore, Piglet gasped with relief. "Mercy me. You frightened me, Eeyore."

"Sorry," Eeyore said gloomily. "I can go away if you like."

"No!" Piglet said quickly. "I'd rather have the company. Being alone can be frightening."

"I suppose so." Eeyore said. "Always found it rather lonely myself. Not that I'm not used to being lonely." He sighed.

Just then, a large raindrop splashed onto Piglet's head, making him jump.

Splash!

Splash!

Splash!

Another splashed into Eeyore's eye. Then there was a rumble of thunder.

"Oh, d-d-dear," Piglet said, feeling frightened once again. "It seems a storm is here!"

Soon, the thunder was crashing and the rain was splashing. Piglet and Eeyore huddled together under a tree.

"Well, I'm glad we're not alone in this storm," Piglet said to Eeyore. "Are you very afraid, Eeyore?"

Eeyore looked at Piglet. "I suppose I am a little," he said. "Mostly just wet though."

Suddenly, Piglet had a thought. "Let's run to Kanga's house!"

The storm was so scary that Piglet didn't really want to
leave the shelter of the tree. But knowing that Eeyore was
frightened, too, somehow made him feel braver.

"Come on, Eeyore!" Piglet shouted.

Eeyore looked dubious. "Are you sure that's a good idea?"

"Don't be scared, Eeyore," Piglet said. "Just follow me!"

Then he dove out into the storm.

With Piglet bravely leading the way, the two friends soon made it safe and sound to Kanga's warm and cozy kitchen.

"What a terrible storm!" Kanga exclaimed.

Roo nodded. "Are you still scared, Piglet?"

Piglet thought about it. "I'm still a very small animal who isn't particularly brave," he said. "But scary things aren't nearly as scary when you have such good friends to be brave with."

Disney
Winnie the Pooh
Roo's Day Away

After breakfast one morning, Roo jumped out of his chair. "May I play in the sandpit today, Mama?" he asked.

"Certainly, dear," she said. "But first you must take your strengthening medicine."

Roo made a face as she spooned the liquid into his mouth. "Blech!" he said. "It tastes terrible!"

"I know, dear. But it will help you grow up big and strong. Now hold still while I wash your face."

"I don't mind being dirty," Roo complained. "Can we go to the sandpit now?"

"In a little while, Roo," Kanga said. "First I need to tidy up the house."

Roo thought the house looked awfully tidy already.

But Kanga swept

and scrubbed

and tidied for what
felt like HOURS.

"Can we go yet, Mama?"
Roo asked **over** and **over**.

Finally, after what seemed like eleventy-million hours of waiting, there was a knock at the door. It was Pooh and Tigger.

"Hallooo, Mrs. Kanga," Tigger said. "We came to see if Roo Boy would like to come out and play with us."

To Roo's delight, Kanga agreed that Roo could go.

"Let's play in the sandpit!" Roo said as soon as he and his friends were outside.

"Hoo-hoo-hoo-hoo!" Tigger exclaimed. "Sounds like a plan to me!

Roo loved playing in the sandpit. First he **bounced** up and down with Tigger, sending sand flying everywhere.

Next he helped Pooh build some very realistic honeypots out of sand.

Finally all three friends lay down and made sand angels.

Tigger led the way to the brook and bounced right into the water. "Come on in, Little Buddy!" he called. "It's much more fun than a bath!"

Roo giggled. "Look out!" he cried, bouncing in with a big splash!

Eeyore wandered over from his house to watch. "Looks chilly in there," he commented.

"It-t-t-t is," Roo said through chattering teeth. "M-m-m-mama always makes sure my bathwater is n-n-nice and warm. But this is still more f-f-f-f-fun!"

Eeyore looked dubious. "Being cold never seemed like much fun to me," he said. "Then again, I'm no expert on it. Fun, that is. Or baths for that matter. Or much of anything, really."

Roo and his friends finished their "bath" in the brook, then rolled in the grass to dry off. That was fun, too!

"Oh, my," Pooh said as he stood up. "All that playing and bathing and rolling has made me hungrier than ever."

"Me, too," Roo agreed.

"Let's go to your house, Little Buddy," Tigger said.

Roo shook his head. "I don't want to go home!" he said. "Mama will make me take my strengthening medicine after we eat. She'll probably make both of you take it, too!"

"Yuck!" Tigger stuck out his tongue. "That doesn't sound very *appa-terizing*. Let's go see if Ol' Long Ears has any grub for us instead."

Rabbit was working in his garden when Roo and his friends

arrived. "Halloooooo!" Tigger cried. "What's for lunch?"

Rabbit frowned. "You two again?" he said to Pooh and

Tigger. "You ate me out of house and home just the other day!"

"Yes, that was us," Pooh agreed. "Your honey was delicious."

Then Rabbit noticed Roo. "Well hello, little fella," he said. "Where's Kanga?"

"At home," Roo said. "Pooh and Tigger are watching me."

"I see." Rabbit rubbed his chin. "Well, Kanga is always willing to help me in the garden, even being as busy as she is. The least I can do is rustle up some lunch for her little Roo."

"And his friends?" Pooh asked hopefully.

Rabbit sighed. "And his friends."

After lunch, Tigger felt a cool wind blow through the Wood.

"Brrr!" Tigger said. "Gettin' chilly out here."

"Perhaps we should take Roo home to get warm," Pooh said.

"I don't want to go home!" Roo shivered. "Maybe Piglet has a scarf I could borrow."

"Good thinkin', Little Buddy," Tigger said.

"Oh, dear!" Piglet said when he heard the predicament.
"Wait right here."

He rushed inside and came back with a warm scarf.

"Thank you!" Roo said. "It's great!"

"It's my favorite. Kanga knitted it for me for my last birthday," Piglet said. "You're lucky you have a mother who can knit you a scarf or anything else, Roo."

"What do you want to do now, Roo?"
Pooh asked.

Roo wasn't sure. He was thinking
about what Piglet had said.
Roo realized he *was* lucky to
have a mother like Kanga.

She always had plenty of
warm clothes for him to wear.

She sang the best songs
to help him fall asleep.

Even though she made him take his strengthening medicine, she also made the best carrot cake in the whole world.

And maybe her baths weren't so bad after all, even if she did scrub his ears a little too hard sometimes.

"I think," Roo said at last, "that I want to go home now."

297

Kanga was hanging out the wash when Roo got home. "I'm back, Mama!" he yelled, jumping to her.

Kanga chuckled. "Did you have fun with your friends?"

"I sure did!" Roo said. He told her all about it while he helped her finish hanging the wash. Then they went inside and had supper, with Kanga's delicious carrot cake for dessert.

Later, Kanga sang Roo's favorite song as she gently tucked him into bed.

Roo soon felt his eyes grow droopy. "Thank you for taking such good care of me," he mumbled. "I love you, Mama."

"I love you, too, dear Roo," Kanga replied.

And the last thing Roo felt was her soft kiss on his head as he drifted off to dream about his busy day away.